C8 000 000 171414

D0581695

Published by Ladybird Books Ltd
A Penguin Company
Penguin Books Ltd., 80 Strand, London WC2R 0RL, UK
Penguin Books Australia Ltd., Ringwood, Victoria, Australia
Penguin Books (NZ) Ltd., Private Bag 102902, NSMC, Auckland, New Zealand
1 3 5 7 9 10 8 6 4 2
© LADYBIRD BOOKS LTD MMIV

Printed in Italy

1844223191

Playtime Rhymes

Illustrated by Lesley Harker

Ladybird

I'm a little teapot

I'm a little teapot,
Short and stout,
Here is my handle,
Here is my spout.
When I see the teacups,
Hear me shout,
"Tip me over and pour me out!"

Teddy bear, teddy bear

Teddy bear, teddy bear,
Turn around.
Teddy bear, teddy bear,
Touch the ground.
Teddy bear, teddy bear,
Climb the stairs.
Teddy bear, teddy bear,
Say your prayers.
Teddy bear, teddy bear,
Turn out the light.
Teddy bear, teddy bear,
Say goodnight.

Round and round the garden

Round and round the garden,
Like a teddy bear.
One step, two steps,
Tickle you under there!

One, two, buckle my shoe

One, two,
Buckle my shoe.
Three, four,
Knock at the door.
Five, six,
Pick up sticks,
Seven, eight,
Lay them straight.

Cobbler, cobbler, mend my shoe

Cobbler, cobbler, mend my shoe,
Get it done by half-past two.
Do it neat, and do it strong,
And I will pay you when it's done.

Two little dicky birds

Two little dicky birds, sitting on a wall,
One named Peter, one named Paul.
Fly away, Peter! Fly away, Paul!
Come back, Peter!
Come back, Paul!

This little pig

This little pig went to market,
This little pig stayed at home.
This little pig had roast beef,
This little pig had none.
And this little pig cried,
"Wee-wee-wee,"
All the way home.

Pat-a-cake, pat-a-cake

Pat-a-cake, pat-a-cake, baker's man,
Bake me a cake as fast as you can.
Pat it and prick it and mark it with B,
Put it in the oven for baby and me.

Dance to your daddy

Dance to your daddy,
My little babby,
Dance to your daddy,
My little lamb!
You shall have a fishy
In a little dishy,
You shall have a fishy
When the boat comes in!

Lucy Locket lost her pocket

Lucy Locket lost her pocket,
Kitty Fisher found it.
Not a penny was there in it,
But a ribbon round it.

Ring-a-ring o' roses

Ring-a-ring o' roses,
A pocket full of posies,
A-tishoo! A-tishoo!
We all fall down.

Oh, the grand old Duke of York

Oh, the grand old Duke of York,
He had ten thousand men.
He marched them up
To the top of the hill,
And he marched them down again.

And when they were up,
They were up,
And when they were down,
They were down,
And when they were only half-way up,
They were neither up nor down.

Pop goes the weasel!

Up and down the City Road,
In and out the Eagle,
That's the way the money goes,
Pop goes the weasel!

Half a pound of tuppenny rice,
Half a pound of treacle,
Mix it up and make it nice,
Pop goes the weasel!

Jack be nimble

Jack be nimble,
Jack be quick,
Jack jump over
The candlestick.

This is the way the ladies ride

This is the way the ladies ride,
Nimble, nimble, nimble, nimble.
This is the way the gentlemen ride,
A gallop, a trot, a gallop, a trot.
This is the way the farmers ride,
Jiggety-jog, jiggety-jog.

The wheels on the bus

The wheels on the bus go round and round,
Round and round, round and round,
The wheels on the bus go round and round,
All day long.

The wipers on the bus go swish swish swish,
Swish swish swish, swish swish swish,
The wipers on the bus go swish swish swish,
All day long.

The driver on the bus goes toot toot toot,
Toot toot toot, toot toot toot,
The driver on the bus goes toot toot toot,
All day long.

Oranges and lemons

"Oranges and lemons,"
Say the bells of St Clement's.
"You owe me five farthings,"
Say the bells of St Martin's.
"When will you pay me?"
Say the bells of Old Bailey.
"When I grow rich,"
Say the bells at Shoreditch.
"Pray, when will that be?"
Say the bells of Stepney.
"I'm sure I don't know,"
Says the great bell at Bow.

Here sits the Lord Mayor

Here sits the Lord Mayor,
Here sit two men.
Here sits the cock,
And here sits the hen.
Here sit the little chickens,
And here they run in,
Chin-chopper, chin-chopper,
Chin-chopper, chin!

One, two, three, four

One, two, three, four,
Mary at the kitchen door.
Five, six, seven, eight,
Eating cherries off a plate.

Little Jack Horner

Little Jack Horner
Sat in a corner,
Eating his Christmas pie.
He put in his thumb,
And pulled out a plum,
And said,
"What a good boy am I!"

One, two, three, four, five

One, two, three, four, five,
Once I caught a fish alive.
Six, seven, eight, nine, ten,
Then I let it go again.
"Why did you let it go?"
"Because it bit my finger so."
"Which finger did it bite?"
"This little finger on the right."

See-saw, Margery Daw

See-saw, Margery Daw,
Jacky shall have a new master.
Jacky shall have but a penny a day.
Because he can't work any faster.

Girls and boys,
come out to play

Girls and boys, come out to play,
The moon is shining bright as day.
Leave your supper and leave your sleep,
And come with your playfellows
Into the street.
Come with a whoop, and come with a call,
Come with a good will, or come not at all.
Come, let us dance on the open green,
And she who holds longest
Shall be our queen.

Notes on nursery rhymes

by Geraldine Taylor (Reading Consultant)

Nursery rhymes are such an important part of childhood, and make a vital contribution to early learning. Collections of nursery rhymes are among the first books we share with babies and children.

Rhyme and word-play help children to recognise sounds and stimulate language development. Feeling and beating rhythm, and joining in counting rhymes encourage early number ideas.

Babies will love to hear you say and sing these rhymes over and over again, and will respond to being gently rocked and jiggled.

Toddlers will love to take part in the actions themselves with lots of clapping, miming and laughing.

The stories and characters of nursery rhymes will fascinate young children. Encourage them to think imaginatively by talking and wondering together about the people and animals. Nursery rhymes are a wonderful source of ideas for dressing-up and story telling.